THERE'S NOTHING *ROMANTIC* ABOUT WASHING THE DISHES

Modern tales with personal magic

Katrina Joyner

There's Nothing Romantic About Washing the Dishes

Joyner, Katrina

Second edition

Published by The Writers of the Apocalypse

117 N Carbon Street, PMB 208

Marion, IL 62959

www.apocalypsewriters.com

Ebook ISBN: 978-1-944322-89-2

ISBN Print: 978-1-944322-07-6

Cover art by Katrina Joyner, ebookcovers4u.com

There's Nothing Romantic About Washing The Dishes

Katrina Joyner

TABLE OF CONTENTS

SILVER

Redemption can come in many ways, depending on how you find it and where you look. For Liz-beth, it comes on the back of the silver mirror that keeps her silver sword.

The last surviving member of The Light spent her Saturdays washing dishes, when she wasn't working, and picking up bits of trash from her cluttered living room floor. Housekeeping was not her strong suit. It never was, she reflected often while leaning against the door frame to her bedroom, trying to figure out which chore needed her most.

Sometimes one has to seek a better way of life, which is how she ended up spending her days doing nothing important. She once thought the simplicity of life with bills and little else would suit her. At the time, she was jaded. Funny, now that she had peace all she could do was long for more.

The telephone rang, the sound muted by a blanket carelessly thrown over it from that morning. By the time the cordless was located, the ringing had stopped. Oh, well. At least it could be put back on its hook, the only bit of consistent orderliness in the house. There it would stay until it rang again, which it did before the hour was up.

"Hey, Liz-beth! Let's go to Central Park." Judy's cheerful voice pierced the earpiece. "It's a record high today; 90 degrees! This calls for a celebration. Besides, you need to get out of the house."

The housekeeper looked out the window at the clear, blue sky. She remembered her long-gone Designation. She once walked proudly down fortress stairways, certain that death was better than peace. Her companions, also members of The Light, had felt that way as well. It was that common belief that held them so close together.

Somewhere in the back of her mind, Liz-beth still remembered their cries in battle. Now the others were gone, and she remained only to clean house and long for those past days. Had she ever noticed the weather before this?

*****Swords flashing, people crying, war chants... banners waving in the wind... and she, thighs girded with weaponry...*****

"Alright," Liz-beth said, forcing herself to sound cheerful. "I'll meet you at the light rail station in thirty minutes."

Judy was a redhead, minus the stereotypical temper, with a perky nose and sparkling green eyes. Even standing behind the train as she was when Liz-beth got there, she could not be missed. She held her straw hat in one hand and, jumping on her toes, waved to Liz-beth with the other. Liz-beth smiled, waving in return. Judy had a way of lightening any mood simply by being there. She seemed oblivious to everything miserable, and that suited Liz-beth just fine.

The two women hugged before punching their tickets. As usual, the 34th Street lightrail station in Bayonne, New Jersey was almost empty. As if Liz-beth's arrival had set the world into motion, the train closed its doors as soon as they boarded. Today it was their private car, smoothly gliding its way towards Journal Square.

Liz-beth watched the terrain whiz by, mentally comparing it to places she had once known. Judy's nose was hidden behind one of her weird books, the one about resurrecting the dead. Liz-beth knew about necromancy and other forms of magic, but seldom paid attention. Privately, she rolled her eyes and grinned.

Judy fancied herself not just a witch, but a sorceress. She obsessed about magic, any kind, and flitted around Liz-beth like a moth to flame. It was magic that had brought them together when Liz-beth befriended the local devil worshippers from sheer boredom. (Judy often said that if it weren't for the devil, they could never have been friends - right before laughing like a maniac at her little joke.)

Judy was incorrigible and wanted to learn everything there was to learn. For Liz-beth, magic was just a matter of breathing; she knew she took for granted the effort others put into learning the arts. When Judy realized what sort of friend she had made, she began to present every occult book in her collection for Liz-beth's opinion. She hoped to one day find something

Liz-beth had never heard of.

Her latest quest, the aforementioned book on necromancy, had been going on for three days. Liz-beth often kept her thoughts private as she was reminded of twisted nights in damp dungeons speaking to the deceased. One such episode had happened when she lived near people who were not as open-minded as Judy. When they had learned of her past (****a *mistake, a stupid mistake while drinking red wine...*****), they burned her at the stake.

Or had it been trial with water? The episodes ran together after a while, like water rushing in streams to join a river.

The train passed the dead tree by the abandoned factory: two landmarks meaning that the couple was halfway there. Liz-beth barely noticed. She had been intimately familiar with such a tree once, and her mind flicked to the remembered feeling of hanging upside down by her ankles. She could almost feel the pressure of the blood rushing to her brain and the pain in her second shoulders. Her twelve kinsmen were dead, the group known as the Light disbanded forever, and she was left to suffer their sins...****

"You're thinking about it again," Judy said, lowering her book.

"What?" Liz-beth blinked innocently, her thoughts scattering as the present came into focus.

"It," Judy said, smirking. "You're thinking about what happened. Don't deny it. I can always tell." Smugly, she buried her nose back into the book.

The train stopped, people got on, and once more they were on their way. Liz-beth's attention wandered outside the car again. She had been hogtied as they carried her home. Someone had broken her wings the day before.

A man walked in front of the procession, his blond hair flashing like gold. He had beaten her, but that was not enough. ****_Her wounds were infected, and her ribs were broken. She was gagged, and every step they took was agony..._****

"Stop it," Judy said, poking Liz-beth's arm.

Liz-beth turned to her friend, surprised.

"I'm not going to let you think about it today," Judy continued, putting her book down with finality. "That's all you do anymore is think about it, and enough is enough. It's time for you to move on."

"I just miss them," Liz-beth said with a melodramatic sigh.

"No, you don't," Judy said, still smirking. "Not them, anyway. Reality doesn't work that way anymore, even if you could get it all back. And if I were you, I'd be glad. There's nothing romantic about being tortured daily for doing what you feel is right."

"There's nothing romantic about washing dishes and making beds, either," Liz-beth complained.

"True," Judy said with a small laugh. "But, didn't you want a simpler, better life? You're damn lucky to be here, you know. Especially you." She waved the book against the world at large. "This place isn't so bad."

At that moment, the train stopped moving and opened its doors. The friends made their way out, heading toward the Path subway station. They were near the water; the sky reflected in the liquid like a photograph. Judy fanned herself with her hat, pausing to admire the view of the Twin Towers contrasting the horizon along the harbor. Liz-beth looked up, and up, into the eyes of Journal Square's landmark; the statue that she liked to call the Impaled Guy.

His uniform incredibly detailed, a World War Polish soldier arched in agony. A bayonet pierced him from behind with its point jabbing towards the sky, accenting the soldier's agonized upward stare. Liz-beth's eyes traced the curvatures of the soldier's right hand, which was contorted.

She was not sure of what the statue was really called, and she barely knew its history. Usually, she read the inscription at the statue's base to remind herself of the story. Today, she chose just to stand and emphasize.

"Always pay homage to the Impaled Guy," Judy remarked sarcastically.

Liz-beth smiled. "It's a beautiful piece of art," she said as her mind flickered to the memory of blood and people crying for mercy. The statue represented all that and more. People were betrayed, Polish citizens died, and all they had to justify it with was a statue standing in a foreign land.

Sometimes, history was frightening. The memory of seeing her people's starving, tortured faces peering out from those cages still haunted Liz-beth. That had been the moment she could take it no more; the cruelty of her purpose became the insurrection of her soul. She would rebel.

*****I hunted you down, but I will set you free. I can never undo my sins, so I will sin to repair the damage instead. I will rebel. I will save you...*

*Her second shoulders stretched, feeling good, as the land fell away beneath her—*****

"Stop it," Judy said.

Inwardly, Liz-beth sighed. Her friend was right, and Liz-beth knew it.

Liz-beth hated taking the subway almost as much as she hated cleaning house, if not more. Self-absorbed people jostled her on all sides, and it was all she could do to keep up with Judy's quick steps. The redhead hummed to herself, smiling alternately at strangers. Liz-beth stood nearby, a silent shadow with her face half-hidden by falling, brown hair.

Memories of victimized crowds pressed Liz-beth as she smiled to Judy's ceaseless chatter. Excitedly, Judy was talking about her book and seemed not to notice that Liz-beth had put herself on autopilot. Judy flipped her book open to the ninth chapter and pressed an illustration into Liz-beth's face. It was a nine-legged demon with a lion's mane and two mouths. Liz-beth pretended to pay attention as Judy described the different techniques to bind the creature.

Liz-beth felt a passing sense of pity for the lion demon. She wondered. If the demon came to a human body, would he regret it after a while? Would he miss his extra limbs, the way she missed her second shoulders, and try to grow his hair wild to replace his mane?

Judy laughed at the idea and suggested they summon him to ask. Other travelers looked at them askance, but Judy never noticed. Liz-beth's memories played like a silent movie inside, always ending with the tree and her ankles in the air as she slowly suffocated.

"Stop it," Judy said, seeming to jump track from demons to Liz-beth's train of thought.

"I'm sorry," Liz-beth murmured. Satisfied, Judy returned to her book.

They exited on 60th Street in Manhattan right at Central Park. Judy took a deep breath and stretched, almost hitting a business man passing nearby. Liz-beth giggled.

"You're wicked," Liz-beth accused her friend. They held hands and walked, ignoring the myriads of people that lounged and talked around them. The babble of multiple languages filled the air. Liz-beth regretted not being able to understand them anymore, then wondered if she would after all this time. Languages changed, as she had, and the old died...

"Oh, please stop!" Judy sighed, shaking Liz-beth's hand. "Look at that, instead!" and she pointed. They were near a big fountain. An angel stepped over the water, oblivious to mere mortals below, and held his arms upward. As usual, Liz-beth followed his sightless gaze and saw only sky.

"I wish," Liz-beth said, "that I were him."

"Or her," Judy said, cocking her head to one side. She never could figure out what sex the angel was supposed to be, or if it had one at all. She claimed it was the robes that threw her off. "Then you'd have the pleasure of being covered in pigeon doo every day. But hey, there are worse ways to make a living."

Liz-beth ran her fingers through the fountain

water, watching the light dance off the ripples she made. "Did you know that water is silver?" she asked.

"No it's not," Judy said. "It's clear."

"It's silver." Liz-beth splashed again. "See?" She giggled as Judy danced, too late, away from flying droplets of water. The sunlight bounced off of each one and reflected in her eyes. Around them, white specks flickered from the moving water. The surface did look silver, if one remembered not to look within. "I like to think of water as the world's best chameleon. Everyone thinks it's clear, but it's really silver."

"I wonder if that's why water can be used for scrying," Judy mused, "like a mirror. You know how all those old mirrors were made with real silver backings. Maybe water is where they got the idea."

"Oh, water is good for a lot of things." Liz-beth shook the liquid from her hand. "Let's go to the waterfall. I'm in the mood to get my feet wet."

"Well spoken," Judy announced. She sang a brief refrain from an old hymn. Liz-beth smiled.

The waterfall, as Liz-beth called it, was a small spring within a group of rocks near the bird sanctuary in Central Park. Not many people frequented that part of the park, almost as if the seclusion were too sacred to disturb. Liz-beth liked to sit in the shade, hidden from view by a leafy bush.

The women could hear the water gurgling before they got there. The happy sound made Liz-beth think of another spring, long ago. There had been a battle, a big one...

*****Their blades rang a final time as she parried clumsily. Her sword flew away, falling into the water, and was lost. Bravely, she ignored the pain in her slashed wrist to stand defiantly against her assailant. Oblivious to the* *drama happening nearby, the others continued to fight around them.*

*"Do it!" she screamed as he hesitated. She ignored the tears in his eyes. "Coward!"*****

"Stop it," Judy said.

The rushing sound of water was all around them now. Liz-beth leaned against a young oak to remove her sandals. The bark rubbed against her skin, but it was not uncomfortable.

"Do you want to talk about it?" Judy finally asked, wrapping her arms around herself. Her book had momentarily disappeared. Liz-beth wanted to ask where it went, but that was one of Judy's secrets. The little woman never seemed to need a backpack.

"Dunno," Liz-beth murmured. She could see the rocks from where she stood. They were just feet away, but Liz-beth sank to the ground to a cross-legged position. "It isn't like its anything you've never heard before."

"I know." Judy sank down beside her friend, throwing a comradely arm around Liz-beth's shoulders. "But spill it anyway. Tell me your story."

"Again," Liz-beth muttered.

"Yes," Judy said. "Again."

Liz-beth sang under her breath while trying to get her thoughts into order. It was an old Norwegian ballad about selkies.

"You should sing more," Judy said softly. "Your voice is like silver."

"Water, you mean," Liz-beth corrected with a faint grin.

She had a sword once; a thing of quicksilver. There were other swords made with ordinary metal, tempered by fire and water. Liz-beth had created her weapon with her soul, using only liquid to give it shape and power. Its blade had shimmered like a new mirror, even on cloudy days. Liz-beth had been very proud of her creation.

."There were thirteen of us," she said after a moment. When she concentrated, Liz-beth could still see their faces. Their eyes looked at her accusingly inside her mind, laying blame on her failure. "And we used to do things for... I guess you can call him God, although it's not what people think it is these days."

"Ha!" Judy barked. "I knew it! Fascist bastards!"

Liz-beth choked on her laughter for a minute. Judy pounded her friend's back. "I made Lucifer die of laughter," she said slyly. "Just wait until I tell the folks back home."

"Stop," Liz-beth said weakly, waving a hand. The laughter subsided, and the two fell quiet. Somewhere above them, a bird hopped on tree branches and threatened would-be invaders.

"I don't understand it," Judy said after a while. "I mean, you were commanded to hurt your own people. You killed them, you made slaves of them, and you generally did things that we consider evil today. THEN," she threw her arms up dramatically, "when you decided to stop it and free everyone, you're the bad guy. It doesn't seem very fair."

"It's not," Liz-beth said with conviction. To make it worse, her lover had betrayed them all. When that final battle came, when the winged hosts opposed them and he turned so suddenly...

***Her sword, flashing brightly as it flew into the water where it had been born...*

Looking up from where she hung into the eyes of the man she loved... The man who asked they let her go, and watched her set free... The searing of pain as whips bit her flesh, the trickle of blood down her back, her cries muted with pain...

Lifetimes being reborn, remembering the day

*she lost a minor war... all for love... the rage at the injustice of it....*****

"I'm just so freaking mad," Liz-beth said suddenly. Tears sprang to her eyes. "Jesus, the man beat me in three seconds flat. And then he didn't have the decency to kill me. No, he had to carry me back home to Papa and show off."

"Yeah," Judy said.

"He said he loved me." Liz-beth dug her big toe into the soft earth. "Puts new meaning to the saying 'you hurt the one you love.'"

"Yeah," Judy said.

"I want my sword back," Liz-beth finished.

"Yeah," Judy said. Wearing a rare, serious expression, she turned to Liz-beth. "You know, that's the first time you've admitted that out loud."

"I know," Liz-beth countered. She had stopped believing in the goodness of God years ago—not that she believed in evil. Long ago, she had only wanted to do what was right. "And it does me no good. I mean look at me... an angel of the Light sitting under a tree in Central Park, wishing she had a sword that was never real to begin with. As if it would make any difference. I'm the only one left; a millennia old scapegoat alive only because she was lucky enough to be betrayed by love. To make matters worse, they can't get my name or the story right. It's messed up."

"Yeah," said Judy.

"My name *isn't* Lucifer," Liz-beth continued. "I'm something more tender than 'light bearer.' At least, my husband thought so. Before he turned on us and turned me in, anyway."

But he had loved her, Liz-beth hoped privately.

Did he hate seeing her on display, or did he thrill when they broke her wings and hung her over the lava pit? She thought sometimes he had been the one to hold the cat of nine tails. She had cried to him for mercy. When she couldn't cry anymore, she begged him with her mind. Once she had reached for a sword that was no longer there and had gotten double the beatings.

"Get over it, Liz-beth," Judy said.

"Someday," Liz-beth said softly.

Her friend hugged her with her one arm, giggling. "This is just so damn ironic."

"And you're too happy."

The water rushed on, oblivious to the women sitting by the tree. And that was life. If she had won that battle, if her companions had survived, life still would have continued. There was no guarantee that Manhattan would have been any different if she had won. Maybe the only difference would be her gloating, rather than moping, over a victory long gone while sitting by rocks that reminded her of it.

The gurgling water made Liz-beth think of swords. Her lover's sword had been shaped of fire. She remembered how their blades had steamed as they met edge to edge in battle. She wondered if the water had absorbed her sword once it fell from her hand.

Not that it mattered, but if she put her hands into water, she could almost feel it lurking there. Judy was correct about reality not working the same as it used to.

Liz-beth stood, brushed the seat of her pants off, and walked to the rocks. The little waterfall, nestled inside, welcomed her like an old friend. She had to walk into the stream to get to it. The crevice was too small to do more than press against, and her feet ached from the searing cold of the water. Liz-beth could hear Judy clambering behind her, opting to climb the rock rather than get wet. Liz-beth reached her fingers into the waterfall, enjoying the sensation of the liquid splashing on her arm.

"Is it still there?" Judy asked.

"Yeah." A mote of light found its way into the darkness of the little cave. It danced down the falling water and disappeared before hitting the creek below. Liz-beth sighed, aware of the hard quality within the fall. There was no pulling her sword out, not ever.

"We should head home," Judy said. "We'll come back again next week. Okay, Liz-beth?"

"Yeah," Liz-beth said. But she continued to poke around inside the tiny cave, feeling the edges of the water, prodding at the energy contained there.

"Stop it," Judy said.

"Alright," Liz-beth said suddenly, backing out of the water and to shore. The women looked at the mouth of the cave, keeping their thoughts as secret as the contents within that darkness. "I'll get it back one of these days," Liz-beth vowed. "And I'll have won."

"You already have," Judy said, surprised.

"What?"

"GEEZ!" Judy laughed a moment. "Don't you get it? You're alive, you're here and now, and okay. So no one remembers what really happened, but you're alive. And no one else is, or if they are they're mindless drones to a system that failed the day you realized how twisted things were. Which is better; the freedom you know or the slavery that is theirs? They didn't break you, Liz-beth, and until they do you will always have won."

Surprised, Liz-beth blinked at her friend. The redhead's speech made sense, too much sense. Pursing her lips, Liz-beth chose not to reply. She put her sandals back on in silence. The deliberate action sent Judy into another fit of laughter.

With that, the women made their way

through the park towards the train station. Central Park sheltered them in green and shade, while the clear sky above slowly grayed with the threat of rain. Judy started to hum.

"Stop it," Liz-beth said.

The song broke off with a startled grunt. "Stop what?"

"Making sense."

Somewhere near Central Park, droplets of silver fell from the clouds to the earth below, like fallen angels seeking a better place to live.

OVER IT

Sometimes when faced with your evil stepmother, leaving bread-crumbs on the trail is not enough. You may have to cross a troll bridge to the other side of your conclusion.

You detest bridges. One the way home from school at night, you try to avoid them but there are only three roads you know. They each have bridges with metal grating and a daunting gap to the water below. So you drive over them as carefully (or quickly) as you can. Behind you, other cars practically ride on your bumper. You think maybe they hate bridges, too.

The worst is when traffic backs up, and you

have to creep over that bridge. You have no car radio. At least the air conditioner works, except the heater is broken. Winter will be coming soon, and jackets are uncomfortable. You glance often at the useless heater lever, wondering what it takes to fix it.

Around you, buildings twinkle like some fairy tale city. There are flashing lights and a siren coming up the bridge behind you. The other cars are already edging aside. Cursing, you veer the steering wheel to the left. Closer to the edge, you eye your rear view mirror to watch the ambulance move past. It finally does, but only after the car in front of you moves up an inch.

Sometimes when driving alone, you fantasize turning your car sharply to the side. You picture the lurch as momentum pushes your vehicle into the clear air. The water would hit with severe brutality, but the car would save you from instant death. Then you would sit, trapped, as water rushes in. Your last moments would be spent gasping with your nose at the roof.

You hate bridges, but you are strangely fond of breathing so you don't take the invisible side road. The traffic finally begins to edge forward until you slide down the other side. Ambulances and police cars are parked at the bottom and up the highway a little ways. There is an accordion which used to be a black truck pulled onto the grass. Several paramedics are clustered around a pale lump of flesh, which does not move.

Trying not to stare, you wonder if it might be someone you know. Speculation takes grip in your mind. What if it's your landlord's bookkeeper? Wouldn't that be nice? You would love to see that bitch prostrate on the side of the road with paramedics futilely trying to keep her alive. Then you wouldn't have to worry about her coming into the house while you're gone. Your belongings would stay put, and she would never again say, "The house is a mess!" because you left a textbook on the table.

Then, if you had something to say to the landlord, you could email him and say it yourself. It would be okay if you occasionally came home too tired to straighten the couch cushions. You grind your teeth as you think about that; how the woman just walks into the house and accuses you constantly of never getting any housework done, even when the only mess is a dirty glass in the kitchen. You hate her for being your landlord's friend, as well as his bookkeeper, and a meddling asshole.

You wonder what it would take to just shove her off of the bridge and be done with.

The flow of traffic speeds up, and your exit ramp comes into view. You take it, going ten miles faster than you should, and glide onto an empty highway. You are eager to get home because your underwear is riding your crotch. Your toes are twisted in a cotton wrinkle of discomfort because your socks are drooping around your ankles. Behind you, the bridge looms forgotten in the night sky.

The next morning, you hit the snooze button as many times as you can. Finally, you throw a pillow at the alarm clock. The clock smashes to the floor, cracking the faceplate and making a continuous, sick sound. If you had super powers, you would throw a fireball at the bloody thing. It would not be a big fireball, of course, because that would burn the house down.

What the hell. You live in Springfield, which burned to the ground at the turn of the 19th century. Your creaky house was built in 1913, after that famous fire. What harm is a little fire going to do, anyway? Maybe Springfield would burn down twice, taking your job and your landlord's bookkeeper with it.

In the mad rush to get away, you are caught in the scramble of panicked citizens as you flee towards the water. Flames are hot on your back while women scream. Idiots jump into the river, which sweeps them away in a swirling current. The bridge is so overloaded with fleeing people, it succumbs and crumbles. Falling bodies tumble downward, pushing each other deep under the water with fatal splashes.

Just as you feel yourself slip downward, you open your eyes and stare at the ceiling. The alarm clock is still screaming, even though you have overslept by two hours. This is the fifth time you have missed work, so you don't even bother to call.

After crushing the alarm clock with your dictionary, the one that was a gift from your ex, you sweep up the pieces to put in the trash.

They never make it there, because on the way into the kitchen you notice your homework on the floor. Without a job, you will finally have time to get things done on time.

Ignoring your homework and the clock pieces now set by the wall, you go back upstairs. You throw away the worn out socks, put on some sandals, and brush your hair. The doorbell rings, but you don't answer the door. The bookkeeper lets herself in, earrings jingling and fingers winking from ridiculous amounts of gold. "Hello?" she carols into the empty front room.

The door shuts; the bitch is inside now, looking at the broken clock pieces and neglected homework. She has a fist on each hip, and her bushy eyebrows are lowered into a straight line. You just know it. She is thinking about calling your landlord to complain. Maybe she will take a picture of the clutter and insist that she can find someone else to house sit while he's on vacation. You want to stomp on the floor hard enough to make the chandelier fall on her head.

She goes into the bathroom, closing the door behind her. Taking this marvelous opportunity, you sneak out the back door and nearly run to your car. Another car almost hits you as you pull out. "Asshole!" you scream, but with the windows up so no one can hear.

There is not much traffic going over the bridge today, so you take it at your own speed. Blue skies span around you, and sunlight glitters on the water like a thousand drowning, burning men. Once you reach the other side, you park your car along the side of the road. That is where you sit for an hour, watching the water. Police cars drive by on the highway, but no one disturbs you.

You wonder what it's like to dance on the

water with the sunlight. The bridge, looming, has no answers for your philosophical query. After a while, you get out of your car and begin to walk. Your feet pass each other, and you are filled with anticipation. Deliberately, you mount the bridge. Your heart begins to pound and you want to turn back, but you keep going.

After a while, your legs tire. The water grows ever more distant, and although you are terrified you continue to walk. Cars sweep by, shaking your foothold. A scream homesteads in your throat, but you don't make a sound. When you finally reach the top, you look down at the water, the dancing lights, and gauge the distance.

If you had three wishes, you would fly. You would turn the bridge into chocolate, or create a working car radio out of thin air. You take a deep breath, leaning over the railing.

"YOU FUCKING BITCH, I HATE YOU!" you

shout. Around you, the echo dances with the lights. You stare at the buildings where you stand, defying gravity. The city stands with you, without pushing back. This is where you stay while the sun moves slowly across the sky.

Finally, you start your descent back to the silent cab of your car. A truck pulls up, and the passenger side window rolls down. Inside, an old woman blinks with bovine eyes. "Are you alright?" she asks. "Did you break down?"

"Nah," you say with a mouth full of teeth. "I just felt like taking a walk."

"Are you sure?"

"Yep," you say while your feet keep moving. The truck crawls alongside of you. "Thanks for your concern, though."

The woman nods after a moment, rolls up the window, and the truck moves away. If you were magic, you would give her a golden goose. Maybe she has a gruff old man at home.

Maybe he makes her bring him beer while he farts and burps in front of the television.

When you finally reach your car, you slip inside and lean back in the seat. There is nothing else you want to do today, but you crank the engine and get back on the highway. The bookkeeper is still at the house when you get home. "Hello!" she says with a smile on her face, thinking about the clock pieces and the homework. Your textbooks and folders are now stacked neatly in a corner, and the pieces are gone. You would have liked to keep those pieces, you decide. "I was just leaving. It looks like the bathroom is finished."

"Awesome," you say, returning her smile with the enthusiasm of an aardvark. "I have to get going to work, or I'd stay to chat. Sorry."

She doesn't mind, in fact she seems relieved. You change clothes in your bedroom, being careful to fold your dirty underwear into a neat triangle and lay it on the pillow of your bed. You hear the door slam, and the house settles back into isolated feeling of emptiness.

For a while, you stand at the window and watch the neighborhood. A dark man pushes a shopping cart down the road. His clothes are murky with filth, and he keeps his eyes to the ground as he walks. You recognize him; he begs for money outside of the emergency room at the local hospital. His cart is empty, but his hands are gripped tightly on the handle as he travels out of your line of sight.

The mattress gives just a little when you sit on your bed. The blankets are rumpled in mountainous heaps, and the pillows need fluffing. You curl between the valleys, your hair becoming a silken river. The phone rings, and you think about your ex. You remember those bottomless brown eyes, dancing as you finished your beer to say, "Lay me another."

You can't remember if you two had sex that night.

The phone stops ringing just before you get up to tear it out of the wall. Once again, things in the house stand still. Outside, someone blows their car horn. The sound manages to get past the window pane, but it's faint when it reaches your ears.

You close your eyes.

GHOST IN THE WATER

When water spirits need rescue, heroes come in many shapes and sizes.

It was steamy hot, but I liked that. Wraithlike, I crept around the pool's edge and watched the swimmers play. Smiling at one bedraggled old woman, I found a seat on the benches. I was too shy to ask anyone if I could share a lane. I felt large and clumsy, so I curled up and tried to appear small.

Somewhere in the back of my mind lurked memories of being able to slip on smaller jeans. Sleek, black dresses hung neglected in my closet. My regalia, too, no longer fit right. This bothered me although I had not been to a powwow in years. Often, I thought of passing my cloth to someone who would honor it. But it took me two years to make the shawl, and the matching skirt represented hours of meticulous beadwork.

So I sat on a bench at the public recreation center, waiting for a lane to clear so I could exercise for twenty minutes. The day before had been easier because the pool was mostly empty. After my workout, a tiny old woman had approached me. She loved long hair, and she wanted to admire my black tresses up close. Used to this, I let her before escaping with a convenient excuse.

Today I waited ten minutes before one of the lanes opened up. Quickly, I slipped into the water. Chills ran up my spine—the water was cold!—and gave me goose bumps. From the corner of my eye, I saw my hair trailing behind like a water moccasin on the prowl.

Slowly, I swam the length of my lane twice before ducking under the water. My leg muscles burned before I stopped. Once again at the pool wall, I stretched and rested. The sounds of the other swimmers surrounded me when I closed my eyes. I smelled chlorine.

"Can I share this lane with you?" a young woman asked. Her honest face made her appear harmless, so I invited her in. Her bathing suit was ripped and tied to keep it in place. Beneath it was another suit, and I wondered why she did not wear just the good one. Maybe she really liked pink.

Before I was halfway across the lane, she passed me and was on her way back. Admiring the contrast between her grace and the clumsy attempts of our neighbors and myself, I paused to watch. Back and forth, she swam without pause. For a moment, I was convinced that she was not breathing.

Maybe she really was an otter; a pink otter with gills. Laughing to myself, I turned to leave and give her the lane. I was tired, and I had to make it home before my daughter returned from school.

"Did you lose a hair tie?" someone asked from my left. Dark brown eyes blinked at me from underneath a swimmer's cap. Their owner looked familiar. "I thought I saw it floating over there. I'll show you."

"Crap," I said, feeling along the length of my hair. "Where is it?"

Brown Eyes pointed, and I started to walk in that direction. As graceful as the pink otter, she swam beside me. I had no difficulty keeping up, but I felt silly walking while she cut swanlike through the water. So I swam, too.

There was no hair tie to be found. Before I knew it, she ducked beneath the lane divider into the shallow area. It was then that I noticed that my hair still was tied. Blushing, I followed her under.

"I thought it was right here," the woman said, confused. She looked around at the floor, feeling with her toes.

"That's okay," I said. "I haven't lost my hair tie after all." I pulled my hair around to show her.

"I only wear black," she responded. "It goes with everything." She described her wardrobe of black and blue pants, some with flowers and some with stripes. Her shirts sometimes had green in them, she explained, but for the most part she liked to dress conservatively. Smiling politely, I edged my way toward the ladder and freedom.

"You weren't born in this country, were you?" she asked suddenly.

"Yes, I was." This, too, was something I had gotten used to. An ex-boyfriend's mother used to argue heatedly with me over whether or not I was Italian. I am not Italian, but trying to convince Isabel was nothing short of a miracle.

"I think I know your mother," Brown Eyes said. "Isn't she Vietnamese?"

Suddenly, I realized that Brown Eyes was none other than my admirer from yesterday. I did not think to wonder why she groped so hard to figure out my nationality. "No," I responded. "My parents are Native American." I took another step towards the ladder.

"You're part White," the lady said. "You're not dark enough to be full Indian."

Despite my inner resolve never to get involved in similar conversations, the innocent statement hit a sore spot. It is a common misconception that all full-blooded natives are dark and wear feathers in their hair. It's also very annoying.

Not all American Indians are dark with

flowing black hair. We don't all keep pintos in the yard (unless that pinto is a horse), and we most certainly don't say "How" to say hello. My father fits the stereotype, but only because he spent every day topless on his shrimp boat for most of his life. Without his pants, he looks like an albino with serious farmer's tan.

I was in the pool to improve my sagging figure, but I remembered a Lakota who once described me as 'a traditional beauty'. Even owing to my Irish ancestor, I never did consider myself to be 'part White'. One simply cannot cut themselves into parts as if they were a pie. My father taught me not to think that way, saying it was against the old ways. So I don't.

This years before my family turned on me, calling me 'White' and 'wannabe'. He pummeled me for pointing out that if I were White, his only grandchildren must also be so. I never quite forgave him.

I looked into the watery eyes of the old woman. "We're paler here on the eastern coast. Think about it: we had tree canopy while the westerners had sunshine." Knowing this was an exaggeration of the truth, I continued. "Some of the old paintings show us as being dark pink." This much I knew because I'd seen reproductions.

"I'm Cherokee and White," Brown Eyes said predictably, conversationally.

Immediately, scores of corrections pushed themselves against my lips. She was either White or Red, I wanted to say, but did not. "Really?" I managed, wondering what time it was. A bruised feeling crept into my chest as if it had been there all along, but I ignored it.

Either red or white... It was my father who carried on the ways through me, and he was Mohegan. But we always had been on our own because the tribe was on the other side of the country. When I grew older and my parents joined a local clan of Cherokee in Georgia, I followed enthusiastically. I drove two hours from my home to the tribal grounds every weekend like a loyal homing pigeon, eager for others of my kind.

The clan mother and I did not see eye to eye, although I was incredibly fond of her. Our biggest argument concerned regalia. Traditionally, a dancer's regalia represents important things to them and their life journey. It is a spiritual statement, and I wanted my dress to reflect my beginning. Clan Mother did not agree. It had to be Cherokee, she said, and I could only use certain patterns and colors... as if I'd actually joined a cult.

One weekend, I arrived early in the morning at the grounds with the beginnings of a shawl and dress. I slept in my car, and when the sun was up I happily bounded out with my cloth clutched to my breast. The old men were up having coffee in the kitchen area, and the women were nowhere to be seen. I got a soda and sat on the railing to talk to them with my outfit by my side.

When the woman I called Cornhair blearily wandered into the kitchen, I scurried to her with a big hug. She pushed me away and told me not to touch her, which was unusual. We always greeted one another with hugs. It was the clan way, I had been told, and although I was not used to being touched I learned to deal.

Eager to show the women my dress, which was a Cherokee tear dress, I waited by the railing. Before long, the chief approached us and greeted the other men. I smiled and waved, but he said, "You, come with me. Now."

Confused, I went with him into the little library that held his office. Every wall was covered in various ethnic objects, including pipes, paintings and a ghost shirt. The artifact that held most of my attention was a war lance affixed over the door. It was adorned in red and was at least an inch thick. I wondered if I could ever learn to use it.

"We've had a meeting about you," the chief said to me. "We've heard that you're part of a Satanic church, and you're not welcome here anymore."

I think my jaw dropped, but the only thing I registered was utter indignation as he repeated himself. "You're not welcome here anymore…"

Three times he said it while looking at me expectantly. Today, I have trouble remembering what I said to defend myself. I denied the charges, of course. They were not, and never have been, true. Later, I learned that the truth was another girl had been accused of the same thing, and she pointed to me to defend herself.

The entire incident reminded me of the Salem witch trials. I wanted to say, "That was very White of you to exile me without giving me the chance to stand up for myself." Rather, I politely rephrased it to a mere sarcastic, "Thank you for giving me the chance to give my side of the story." Using the word 'White', although a well-placed insult at the time, would have served no good purpose.

I was escorted off of the grounds, never to return. When I told my parents of the betrayal, they weren't even aghast. Deep inside, I had expected them to defend me in some way, but they never did. Rather, they chose to side with the tribe and call me a witch.

A sweat lodge was erected in the back yard one day. Mother forbade me to go near it or even to go into the back yard. Finally it was apparent that they valued their new religion over their only daughter.

As time passed, they grew closer to the Cherokee clan while I found myself increasingly estranged. These days I cannot refute that this clan is more like a cult to me than not.

Unaware of my inner conflict, Brown Eyes gossiped about African Americans and how the Laundromat owner accused her of dating them. I wanted to interject that my boyfriend was mulatto, and that when you looked at the entire history of mankind, there was no one, pure race. Rather than waste the effort, I remained silent.

The accusation had taken place in front of Brown Eyes' husband, the tale went on, and if it were not for them moving into a different dump from where they currently lived. She never went back to that Laundromat, and she never would.

"At least you have a dump," I said, taking the change of subject and going with it. At home, I lived with my parents while recovering from another failed relationship. My daughter had the only spare bedroom to herself, my son lived with his father, and I slept where I found a free corner. I was either at work, off with my daughter, or in the bedroom; the family rarely saw me. When they did, we rarely spoke.

I was nothing but a ghost—a ghost who stood trapped by conversation at the public pool. A ghost that wanted the past to let her go.

Nodding, Brown Eyes agreed with me. She still remained completely oblivious to the tortured memories she had kicked awake to haunt me. "So many out there don't have any place to call their own," she said. "But, you should get going. I don't mean to make you late for anything."

At last. Gratefully, I made my way out of the pool and to the showers. I wondered if the Cult would be holding their annual powwow, and I reminded myself that I would never go to it again. I grabbed my brush from my locker and found a mirror.

The chlorine did my hair no justice, and it hurt to brush it. I cursed frequently. "Are you okay?" asked a young woman as she entered the room. She carried a brown backpack and had the same figure I hoped to regain someday. Her hair was a luxurious golden brown with just enough curl to look heavenly.

"The chlorine makes my hair impossible to brush," I explained with a grimace.

"Try conditioner," the girl said. "I have a bottle if you'd like to borrow some." She pulled a green bottle from her backpack and handed it to me. It was the spray conditioner, the kind you leave on. Curiously, I sprayed it on my hair and gave an experimental swipe with the brush.

Smooth as silk, the brush slid through my hair. Triumphantly, I brushed until I had my hair once again in order. "That does make a difference," I said to her. "Thank you!"

She smiled. "No, don't mention it." She went about her business now that her good deed was done. I scampered to my truck in the parking lot. Crows sat on tree branches and car tops, calling to each other. One got very close to me and cocked his head to the side.

How appropriate, I thought. Carrion eaters looking for food were looking at me. Grabbing the camera from my truck, I stalked the black birds. As if they knew what I was trying to do, they flew out of reach and cackled to each other.

One bird did assent to sit on my truck and pose. A single shot later, he flew away to join his brethren. I gave up on picture taking and put my camera away.

My mind flicked briefly over Brown Eyes, but it lingered on the girl in the showers. If crows eat the dead, and memories torture them, then perhaps angels provide the means to work things out. Like with ghosts, one does not always realize what they're dealing with until after the incident is over.

Tomorrow, I decided, I would bring conditioner.

THE GLASS OF CAPPUCCINO

Your fairy godmother may be closer than you think, and her motives may not be so easy to understand.

"**Y**ou have a boyfriend, don't you?"

It was an innocent question accompanied with curious brown eyes and a familiar smirk. Paul glanced back down to his cappuccino, obviously thinking about Jason. The two had gotten into a fight recently, and he was sharing his woes with Linda. Linda, startled at the question, stopped mid-sip into her diet soda.

"Nah," she said casually after swallowing

slowly. "Hell, just listening to you complain about Jason makes me want to swear off love forever." She flashed him a smile of her own. "I can't believe he was such a jerk last weekend."

"I suppose," Paul recanted. "I guess I shouldn't have yelled at him in the parking lot, either."

"There's my guy," Linda giggled. "No wonder Jason puts up with you."

Paul, lost in thought, picked up his spoon and dipped it into his drink. It was chocolate covered, a treat that Linda could only savor with her eyes because she was allergic. She reflected that it was much like the other treat, the one that actually held the spoon. Paul was a handsome man.

She envied Jason, and Paul knew it. The two had come to terms with the situation months ago, at the beginning of their friendship. It was also why Linda had been startled by Paul's inquiry. Did he actually expect her to have a boyfriend, caught as she was? Suddenly, she very much wanted a cigarette.

Fag hag. The word echoed in her mind automatically. Someone had called her that the other night when she was out dancing with the gang from work. She was a fag hag because she loved Paul who loved another man. It was a cruel word, one of many she had encountered through the years. It only bothered her because of the division; how it pushed her feelings from the truth. She loved Paul because he was a wonder among men, and as a result she accepted him for whom and what he was. She did not expect him to love her in return.

Paul had stopped playing with his spoon to take another drink from his cappuccino. He said, "And I guess he had every right to be upset over the telephone call."

Playfully, Linda put her chin in one hand to

regard her friend. "Don't forget the flat tire."

"That wasn't my fault!" Paul protested.

"So it was someone else who didn't pick up those nails from the driveway?"

"No, but I...!" Paul sputtered and threw straw paper at her. "It wasn't my fault!"

Linda giggled again. She took a deep drink from her glass, watching Paul from over the rim. His eyes danced as they did when the two bantered. "Okay," she said softly, "we'll blame it on the dog."

"We don't own a dog," Paul said.

"All the better."

The two shared another grin, an evil one. The waitress stopped by their table. "Do you need anything else?" she asked them in a sweet voice, the kind waitresses the world over use when hoping for a big tip. "Miss, do you need a refill?"

"No, thank you," Linda said. "I'm fine."

The waitress walked away. Linda watched the swing of her hips for a second before turning her eyes back to Paul. Paul, who had caught the look, said, "She's pretty."

"If you like the type," Linda observed. Involuntarily, she sighed and took a bite from her bagel. That was the way of it. You were either the type or you were not. In Linda's case, she was usually not the type.

Boyfriend indeed. Who on earth would have her? She thought of a conversation from two years ago that touched on the very matter. Back then she was engaged to the jerk of jerks. When asked why she didn't leave her fiancé, she'd said that no one else would have her. People assumed the fiancé had led Linda to believe this. This was not true, of course. Linda had come to the conclusion on her own.

Jason is a fool, Linda thought. For a moment, she hated him. As far as she could tell, nothing Paul ever did was good enough for Jason. Poor Paul spent most of his time frustrated over something Jason was overreacting to. The rest of his time, he spent it frustrated at something Jason had said or done. There were times that Linda just wanted to smack Jason. There were other times she just wanted to hug Paul and take away his pain. And then where were times...

"What about Benjamin?" Paul asked suddenly, obviously jumping back to his question. Benjamin, another co-worker, had recently asked Linda out. She thought that he was okay, but it bothered her when he talked about sex as if that would actually interest her. She'd never given him a direct answer because it seemed silly to turn men down just because she had feelings for Paul.

"Eh," she said flatly. "I might go out with him this Friday. I haven't decided yet."

"He's a nice guy," Paul said.

"I know." The waitress walked by again, so Linda asked her for some cream cheese. The couple sat in silence until the cream cheese was delivered. Linda fiercely smeared her bagel with it, singing eerie movie music and muttering about space ships. This earned a hearty laugh from Paul. Mission accomplished, Linda took another bite from her bagel.

Sure Benjamin wanted her. What troubled her was *how* he wanted her. In that respect he was worse than her ex-fiancé, who never never touched her. When she ran out of money he threw her out of the house. In fact, the ex-fiancé spent a considerable amount of time reassuring Linda how ugly she was.

Benjamin, gods bless his honest soul, just wanted to get laid. When he set eyes on Linda, they were full of lust. She'd seen him cast the same look on the other girls at work as well as a few of the men. Still, he was also the first man in years to ask her out. Memories echoed from high school: a guy saying, "I don't want to date a fat chic!" Lust was all about looks, and Linda's looks weren't exceptional.

It wasn't that lust was anything she'd never encountered before, but it was something she didn't care to deal with. She was a grown woman, and some tiny germ of self esteem told her that she deserved better. The problem, she told herself for the hundredth time, was that her idea of better was a gay man. It was ironic. Straight men didn't want her because she wasn't pretty enough. Paul didn't want her because she wasn't man enough.

"Damn Jason," Paul muttered, taking his last drink of cappuccino. He signaled the waitress for another cup, which was delivered with speed.

"It's not your fault," Linda said soothingly.

The waitress walked by again, this time ignoring them for the table nearby. Paul barely glanced at her. Linda involuntarily wondered if he thought of her as a fish.

Fish was another word, one that had been thrown her way many times by her older brother's boyfriends. It was the cruelest word of all, in her opinion, and it didn't strike her as fair. She certainly didn't spend her time thinking of mean things to call men of any sexual persuasion. She didn't deserve to be cut down in the same way.

Paul leaned back in his chair to regard his friend. "I think you should go out with Benjamin," he announced. "Give him a chance."

"I might," Linda muttered. She didn't want to give him a chance. She was very uncomfortable with the thought. She wondered why she couldn't fall for a straight guy, then remembered all the unrequited times she had. The more things change, the more they stay the same. She wanted to cry, but instead she balled the paper from her straw and threw it at Paul. Paul dodged nimbly before picking it up to throw it back at her. He was smiling.

Linda spent a lot of time thinking of ways to make Paul smile. When they'd met, she noticed right away that his smiles were no more real than silk flowers in a graveyard. She spent a lot of time thinking of new things to show him or jokes, even amusing letters that she slipped onto his desk at work. With each genuine smile, her spirit soared. Paul deserved to be happy. It made her feel good when that happened.

Someone walked into the cafe. The movement caught Linda's eye, but it wasn't anyone she knew. She turned her attention back to the rest of her bagel, which she finished delicately. Paul was eating his own bagel, sans cream cheese, and still wore his smile. She hoped it would last.

She should date Benjamin. She felt her gaze soften as she studied the curl of Paul's hair and the line of his nose.

Paul was not aware that she was studying him, as he was looking at something across the cafe. His Adam's apple bobbed as he swallowed. The twinkle in his eye had not died, so Linda knew that he wasn't thinking of Jason again. He was merely observing their environment.

Linda drank the last of her cola, wishing she were someone else. She wished she were a guy. Then maybe someone would love her.

It seemed to her that men suffered being an object a lot less than women. What was it that her ex-fiancé had told her? Oh, yes. That she was no one in particular, and as a woman she didn't deserve to think. Sometimes - hell, most times - she believed that. No one expected her to think, just to do her job and get out of the way.

Except Paul. Unlike any of the straight men she had ever dated, Paul was her best friend. He liked to see her smile; liked to hear her thoughts. He liked how she made him think. When he hugged her, she was enveloped with warmth she had never felt before. She felt safe in his presence. He was strong to her; she'd seen him break up a bar fight once. He had been a veritable junkyard dog that night. Standing on the sidelines, she'd been torn between protecting him and feeling pride that he would do such a noble deed.

Well, Paul was Paul. She loved him because he was Paul. It was wrong to expect him to be anything more than that.

She put some money down on the little table. "It's time we went to work," she said reluctantly. It wasn't that she hated her job. She didn't want to leave the cafe with Paul. "It sucks, but there it is."

Paul's grin did not fade. "Do I get a happy note today?" he asked in his boyish way.

Linda grinned, despite herself. "Oh, yeah!" She pulled it from her purse and tossed it at him. "You can't read it until we're in the office."

"Awwwww," Paul said, tucking the note away in his pocket. The notes had become a tradition to which he looked forward to. Today's edition was a joke she had found on the internet.

The two left the cafe arm in arm, giggling when Linda stumbled on her own heels to crash into Paul. The waitress claimed their payment as quickly as she could and was gratified to see that Linda had left her a huge tip. Outside Paul and Linda walked by the cafe window to Linda's car. They got inside and drove away.

Paul's cappuccino glass, carried away by the waitress as she cleared the table, had only been half empty... Or half full, depending on which of the two would have been looking at it.

FOR FEAR OF BREAKING HEARTS

Fear can do more than hold you back.

It was a Saturday; one of those bright and glorious days in which you wake up feeling good to be alive. The children were at their father's house for visitation and (bonus) it was my day off. I had no alarm clock set.

I lazily opened my eyes and for a moment contemplated the ceiling and the glory of a quiet, Spring morning. I swear to you there were birds singing. Off in the distance, Pan was probably playing his pipes gently in tune with

Ode to Spring. This was going to be the kind of day young mothers learn to appreciate. I was going to clean house, maybe paint something, and watch TV. This was the life.

. After waking up on my own terms, I rolled out of bed in no rush. I puttered across the kitchen still wiping sleep from my eyes as I made way to the bathroom for the first morning ritual. Through the windows I could see the flourishing green of the foliage that burst happily around the area outside. I still remember the beams of sunshine that cast their way across the kitchen floor. The pile of dishes still in the sink.

The house I lived in was an old farmhouse located in the middle of a forest made up mostly of mimosa and forgotten pecan trees. It even had a rusting silo and burned out horse stall in the far back of the yard. My destination, the bathroom, was very tiny the way old bathrooms tend to be and attracted moisture. If the house were picked up by aliens and set down in the middle of the Sahara Desert, after fifty years the bathroom would still be wet enough to raise guppies. This meant it had a slight mold problem, because if there's one thing mold loves it's the dark, wet stuff of bathrooms. I often left the bathroom window open to let in fresh air and discourage the growth of mold.

After a while, whether you realize it or not, you come to expect your bathroom to feel a certain way. Either you feel something is missing because the stink of too much bleach isn't burning your nostrils or, in my case, you step into that cool, moist room ready to do your business and get out as quickly as possible. I fully anticipated the morning air to greet me as soon as I opened the bathroom door, like an old friend. The solitude that room offered was just something I had come to expect. I completely took it for granted, as a matter of fact.

This picturesque routine came to an abrupt halt the minute I opened the bathroom door. I think I stood there just long enough to register that things weren't how they were supposed to be before backing away carefully, closing the door, and walking back into the kitchen. My mind had to back up a bit to comprehend what I had just witnessed.

This was beyond belief, and I knew it. So I did what any confused storyteller would do. I picked up my phone to call someone, because I had something really weird to tell them. It was the only method I had to wrap my brain around the change in my morning plans. The only person home that morning was my best friend.

"Hey," I said a little breathlessly, squishing greeting formalities into the shortest word possible. "My bathroom is full of bees."

That's right. Bees. I don't know when or from

where, but a swarm of honeybees had decided to, well, swarm. Maliciously they had made their way through the window into bathroom and had patiently waited for me to fall into their trap. It was downright nefarious.

"Your bathroom has what?" my friend asked, not because she was hard of hearing. Let's face it. When you wake up to find your bathroom is full of bees, it's a little unbelievable.

"Bees." I'm sure you can feel the hair at the nape of your neck rise at the mere thought. After all it's common knowledge that bees are probably the most vicious of land insects, after wasps. Spiders don't come in at the top of the list because they're not technically insects. And roaches are gross but will only scare you when you realize they can fly.

I honestly can't remember most of our conversation. It must be because the shock hasn't worn off after all these years. I'm pretty sure my friend took a moment before asking me, "What are you going to do?" (Then again she might have laughed and told me to sober up. Who knows.)

"I don't know," I probably replied. "What would you do?"

"Kill them of course!" Again, this is but a speculation on the conversation.

I couldn't do that. Sure these dangerous monsters had taken over the back of my house and ruined my sense of solitude, but if anything I wasn't prone to bee murder. In fact, in case of zombie apocalypse I'd probably be one of the first people to die. I'm positive you can out walk a shambling zombie, but they don't give up where you as a mere mortal will eventually get tired. Then the crucial moment would come—that moment in which you have to choose between shooting your dead grandmother in the face with your gun or getting out alive. I couldn't do it; not completely because I'd probably miss or would have no ammo.

"Maybe there's another way," I might have said. I know I at least thought it to myself on some subconscious level. Nowadays if this happened to me and I called my best friend for advice, she would instantly open an internet search browser to look it up. We probably would discuss the anatomy of bees, their mating habits, and finally move on to finding numbers for beekeepers that specialize in capturing swarming honeybees. Sense of panic? Not in the face of Google, never.

This inauspicious incident, however, happened before I really knew what the internet was. I'm pretty sure it was before a lot of people knew what the internet was. My phone was a wall phone with a cord long enough for me to walk to town and never lose my phone connection. Any computers I had seen up until that day had black and white or green screens, and my brother referred to some of them as "Trash 80's." So my friend was at a loss with no resources at her fingertips, although she did find it a little funny.

I didn't talk to her long, because there were bees in my bathroom. Whatever else we may have chatted about, after a little while I let her off the phone and returned to the issue at hand. This was a matter of national security. My home had been invaded by six-legged terrorists of the honey making variety. I found that a little distracting. I paced the house, wondering what to do. I couldn't go to the bathroom without, I was sure, getting stung. I could ignore it, except it was an entire swarm of bees in my bathroom.

My beautiful lazy morning had been turned into the stuff of Hitchcock nightmares. Fortunately for me the bee bathroom trap had failed, but the bees held my bathroom hostage. They were not planning on releasing it, I could tell. There would be no negotiations.

I have to reiterate, because I just don't get the sense that you understand the import of what I'm saying. My bathroom was filled with a swarm of honeybees. They were everywhere, flying in a darting mass. You could hear their soft hum at the door as they went back and forth trying to find a way out. You could sense their tiny feet walking all over the sink, bathtub and commode. You could feel them waiting for you to come closer. Waiting. I, the eternal coward, was more than willing to let them keep waiting.

The bathroom window was right there, wide open as could be, but we have all seen insects when they get trapped in the house I'm sure. The suckers flutter all over the ceiling, your glass of milk, and everywhere else looking for the way out. They fly right by the open door and choose the opposite direction just to drive you crazy. Somewhere their bug buddies are keeping score to see who can make the human go nuts the fastest. The more suicidal of these bugs will dive at your face.

For these bees, I also suspect that to go out the window would have meant to backtrack. These were clearly forward thinking bees that could only go one direction, and that meant they were stuck in that tiny little room.

First order of business for me was to go to the store, use the bathroom, and make my way back to the house. I may also have bought something to eat, because having bees in your house discourages using the stove that's set too close to the bathroom door. After that was done, I could think a little more clearly but it wasn't enough. I wasn't terrified of the bees so much as extremely wary and afraid of being stung. Okay and maybe I was scared.

I wanted to get them out of the house. The only way I could think to do that was to coax them out somehow. What do you do when a wasp is stuck in the house? If you're compassionate you open a window. What do you do when a fly is in the car and it's too fast to kill? You open the window before the dreaded monster can attach itself to your face and use it's alien tongue to suck up your brains. It's common sense.

In this case, the window was already open. The next time I checked on the bees, a large amount of them had found their way back out the window to continue their journey. There were still a lot left. These probably were the stupid ones: The ones that couldn't find their way out of a wet bathroom. Indeed, they were not doing that. I had to find another way for them to leave.

The layout of the house offered a possible solution. If you stood in the bathroom door looking out, you directly faced the back room. It was really a little utility room that probably was meant to be a washroom at some point. I used it to store my comics.

Directly across from where the bathroom door was the backdoor. This door, when opened, gave access to the most gloriously green backyard any country house hoped to offer. It had accidental wild tomatoes, wild flowers, and occasional cat offerings of bunny and mouse. More importantly it had the blue sky and open air. It was Narnia and the real world rolled into one.

The bathroom door and the back door may have been directly in line to each other, but to a bee they may as well have been miles apart. Still it was something. Maybe, I thought, I could get the bees to leave that way.

I felt like it was the only hope I could offer in the moment. It's not like I could call the Bee Busters up to exterminate the bees with their special equipment. There were no little bee taxies to call, and I may already have suggested offhandedly what a coward I am. This plan had to work.

First, I opened the back door as wide as it would go and propped it open with a bit of broken brick. Then I made my way back to the bathroom door and the room filled with swarming, evil rage. You could almost feel the bathroom door tremble as it barely held back the maleficent force trapped inside. Before I could change my mind, I opened the bathroom door wide. As fast as I could, I fled back into the safety of the kitchen and waited.

You know how in the old cartoons, bees band together in a solid shape of dots and take off without a backward glance? At the very last, they'll form the shape of a thankful thumbs up in situations like this before they completely depart. This did not happen. That's about as accurate as putting a flame to a mercury thermometer to fake a fever. (Don't try that, by the way. It doesn't end well.)

I'm not sure what I was expecting to happen. There was no thank you shaped mass of bees flitting out the back door to the wild blue yonder. Rather, as I stood helplessly watching in the kitchen, they sensed the light coming in through the back door in groups. Two or three would fly out at a time into the back room. Slowly the remaining bathroom swarm became a back room swarm.

They had left the bathroom, but only about half left the house. The back door stood there, enticingly open, but these bees were relentless. They knew I wanted them gone. So some decided the easy path I provided wasn't good enough. Another opportunity had seemingly presented itself.

In the middle of the bees' path from bathroom to freedom was a small window; the kind with the wooden squares and the old windowsill. Wouldn't you know it, but the light coming in from that window summoned them to it and that's where they stayed. My back room window was now decorated in vicious, frantic honeybees. I think it's safe to say they were none too pleased that they had been fooled.

The window had lied to them. It teased them. There they were, given a view of the glorious outdoors but the clear glass refused to let them pass. Repeatedly they beat their little bodies against the windowpane trying to get out and into the freedom of the beckoning sky.

By then I started to get a sinking feeling in my chest. I felt helpless as I watched from a distance, unsure of what to do. I didn't dare get too close to these murderous, dangerous insects.

I hoped maybe they'd see the open door and went about my business for a little while. Being distracted by the thought of my surprise guests, this didn't turn out to be as much as it originally might have been. I kept finding my way back to that window to see the plight of the bees trapped there. They were desperate, I knew they were desperate. I was too afraid to get very close, but from my distance I could tell that some were no longer flying against the windowpane. They were walking along the bottom sill, back and forth.

What was wrong with them? I couldn't understand it. I had tried calling the other few people I knew but no one was home to hopefully give me answers. It was just me and the bees. The number of bees had dwindled a little, to be sure, but the ones trapped by the light of the window were never going to leave.

I gave up on getting anything done. I stood in my kitchen watching this, feeling anxious. If they didn't sting me, I thought, they were sure to sting my children when they came home. I didn't know that much about bees.

Sometime in the afternoon I got brave enough to return to the inner recesses of the back room. About two dozen bees had not left. They tried—oh how they tried—but they were fixated on leaving through the window. By this point in time, I had stopped viewing them as a dangerous threat to the world and all humanity. I could see how trapped they were. I knew to be wary of them, and I was still afraid, but they were simply trapped. All they wanted was out.

Just then, I had a genius thought! There was a kernel of hope. Somewhere in the heavens, some deity had stretched out their mighty hand to touch my craven little brow and said, "YOU

SHALT THINK. AND IT SHALL BE GOOD."

That's right. I decided I would try to open the window.

This was no ordinary idea. I knew that accepting this mission could mean certain harm to my tender flesh, but I was the only one there that could possibly do this. There was no time to make my peace with the universe. I had to go in now. The fate of the bees rested on my shoulders.

I took a step, then another. Before I knew it, I was right there by the window practically on top of the bees. They seemed so small, for such wicked creatures. Some of them were buzzing up the windowpane to the top of the bottom half of the window, and others were content to cling to bits of the window frame.

Deftly I maneuvered my body so that I was arching around the window in the best possible position to make a quick escape. The bees didn't notice me. So far so good.

The next part was a little tricky. I had to reach my hand into the bees' space to grab the window lock. That took a couple of tries, because one of the bees decided to crawl over it at the wrong time. Finally I unlatched the lock, very carefully. The bees continued to ignore me. Or maybe they didn't care.

Now that I was in position and had the window unlocked, it was the moment of truth. It was time to push the window open.

This window was the kind that slide the bottom half up. Opening it too quickly could squish a bee between the wood frame and window, or at the very least arouse the bees into their special kind of anger and make me regret my moment of compassion. I had to slide it slowly up. At least there was no screen on this window, I thought, because I wouldn't have been able to take that off. So far so good.

I carefully placed my hands on the window and pushed up.

It didn't budge.

I pushed again. Nothing moved.

I took a closer look at the offending window. It was painted shut.

I had faced other painted windows in that house before, and I'd managed to get them to open. So I kept trying. When that failed, I got a butter knife and carefully plucked at the areas where paint had made its way around the window frame to seal it shut. I broke a butter knife, but I could not get the window to release its hold.

I retreated to the safety of the kitchen. The only other thing I knew to do was to catch the bees in containers and let them go outside, the way you would catch and release a spider when you don't want it to rain. The problem with that is while catching one bee to release outside, I might upset the rest of the bees. These are bees we're talking about here. Scourge of the universe, next to wasps in case you forgot.

The gods were not forthcoming in any further ideas. By this point, most of the bees had stopped flying and were either dead or nearly dead on the windowsill. There were a few still flying, but their movements were sluggish. Others walked around, still looking for a way out but not doing much more than that.

I knew the bees were dying—it was obvious—but I couldn't understand how. It had only been a few hours, and I had never seen bees die so quickly in my life. I did the only thing I had left to do.

I phoned my father.

Let me tell you about my dad real quick. He's full of all sorts of awesome tidbits of knowledge. He's swam a river of piranha, lived through hurricanes, and married a headhunter. (Not my mother.) He has faced down thugs with a flare gun, gotten caught up in the Siege at Wounded Knee, and swears he used to work with Dolly Parton before she got so famous. As a child I had this image of my father in the jungle being chased by Nazi Germany, or perhaps he was a time traveler from the Wild West. As far as I was concerned, even standing in my kitchen as a grown woman, my father knew simply everything.

Besides and most importantly he used to be a beekeeper.

I had tried to call him that morning but he wasn't home. Who knows where he was at the time—slaying a dragon somewhere probably. I had to try him again and hope against all hope he was there. For the third time that day I dialed my father's home phone number. I was praying, *praying,* he was home.

I don't know why I cared so much about

these dodgy insects stuck in the back room of my house. I know that someone else would have unceremoniously went to their bedroom, dialed a special number on a hidden number pad just inside the bedroom closet door, and Batman's butler would appeared from within a secret hallway. He would have handed them the flamethrower to end all flamethrowers. Then with just as much relaxed candor, this someone else would have used that flamethrower on those bees *without lighting the curtains on fire.*

In fact nothing else in the house would have caught on fire. Just the bees. They would just be that good.

I do not have Batman's butler hiding in a secret hallway. I only had my phone, and I was in luck. My father was home. He answered the phone with his lazy, "Hello."

I blurted to him, "Dad. My house is full of bees!"

"What?" he asked, although I'm not sure if he didn't believe me or if he just didn't hear me right. It's hard to tell with him.

"A swarm of bees came in through my bathroom window," I said.

"A swarm of bees came in through your bathroom window," my dad repeated, which I suspect is his way of digesting the gist of the problem. "What are they doing coming into your window?"

"I don't know, Dad!" I exclaimed. "But they've been in the house all day. I managed to get some to go back out the back door, but there are some that are by the window in the back and I can't get the window open."

"You can't get the window open."

"They aren't flying anymore, Dad."

"They're not."

"I don't know why but they're all dying and my house is being littered in dead bees."

"That's because they're dying," Dad said.

"What??" I knew they were dying. It was obvious my bees were sort of solving my problem by themselves, but it still hadn't quite registered until that moment. "But why, Dad?? They've only been in here for a few hours. I haven't poisoned them. I've got doors open so they can escape. Nothing has harmed them."

This is when my father told me something that I'll never forget. To this day I still remember his voice on the phone and my shocked reaction when I heard him, how my eyes darted back towards the room where the tragic scene had been playing out for hours. "They have broken hearts," he said.

"I don't understand," I stuttered.

"They're cut off from their queen," my dad explained. "It's getting dark and they can't get to her. Their hearts are breaking from this. So they're laying down to die. If honeybees get separated from their queen, they die of sorrow."

This was a lesson of the birds and bees that I had never expected in my entire life. These terrible monstrous attack kamikazes of the insect world had accidentally been left behind by their queen when they had invaded my territory. It had been a long day trying to find the way back to their queen mother, but now the day was nearly over. Monsters have hearts, hearts that break very easily. Monsters are small and fragile. Monsters will easily give up and die when the sun goes down.

"What do I do?" I asked.

"There's nothing you can do," Dad said to me. "The day is almost gone." With that last piece of wisdom, the conversation was over.

In that moment I no longer saw the bees as liver-eating baby Cthulu monsters from the deep dark hive. They were sad little beings that I had allowed to die in my fear and ignorance.

After I hung up the phone, I paced around the door to the back room trying to figure out what to do. I was still afraid, but I couldn't just give up now that I knew the truth.

If I could just get the courage to actually help the bees by handling them, they might sting me and then they would die anyway. I couldn't open the window. It was stuck permanently. They were never going to see the back door waiting for them, even though it was only two feet away. The light outside was dying as the sun got closer to sunset.

I took a close look and there were only four bees left alive. Two were laying on their sides on the windowsill, one was walking around and the other stirred a little. All of the rest were dead.

In a cosmic sense, it was my fault.

My cowardice and inaction had killed them.

Guilt is a powerful emotion. It sits in your

chest and kicks at your heart while muttering angry things like, "Like that? Eh? Want some more? I'll give you some more, you heartless jerk. Take this. And this. And this!" It sometimes doesn't let go even after we find closure.

We do all sorts of things because of guilt. The reason why I couldn't bring myself to exterminate the bees in the first place is because of guilt. I had killed a crab at the beach when I was small and still remember how I felt. It's very hard for me to so much as consider doing anything like that again.

Guilt mingled with pity can be even more uncomfortable. When mingled with pity, guilt suffuses your entire soul to the point that you almost forget to breathe. Your mind freezes and your heart squeezes in just the right way to motivate you to do something to alleviate the pain.

In my fear I had let all of these little spirits die

in my home.

All they wanted was to get to their queen mother, to go home, and I had spent the entire day pacing my house in wary caution. Too much caution.

I had taken away their freedom in the name of safety.

I was a coward and a jerk.

There was only one thing left to do, and I had to do it or be dammed forever as the monster I truly was. After a quick search I found a piece of paper. I approached the windowsill where the last little women prepared to give up the ghost. They weren't aware of me, and I finally realized that they probably never knew I was there all day. I looked down on them, wishing I'd been brave enough to do this sooner.

Gently I scooped them onto the paper. The one with the most strength left tried to crawl away, but she didn't make it very far. Soon I had all four survivors on the paper. I turned towards the back door.

I had to walk carefully so as not to drop any of my tiny passengers.

So there I stood at my backdoor holding a piece of paper with four worn out bees on top. Maybe I was too late, I was thinking, but if nothing else they could die free outside.

In this moment, the universe provided a miracle.

When the light outside and the air hit them, the bees stirred. It was like they lifted their tiny heads and saw the wide world around them. With the paper still in my hands, I watched the strongest of the four fan her wings to life and lift herself in the air. Slowly she flew out of sight.

Then the second strongest realized she was outside and started to move her wings. As this was happening, the other two were coming back to life. The second lifted off from the paper and into the air just as the third started to fan her wings. Before I knew it she was also flying away. That left the last and weakest of them.

I set the paper down on the step, feeling sure that I was too late for this one. I looked away for just a moment. When I looked back, it was just in time to see her lift off. She flew away in the same direction as her sisters towards her new home.

I still want to cry when I remember those bees. In fact, I'm tearing up just a little as I tell you this story. I probably will never let go of the guilt, and I don't want to.

This was probably one of the most important lessons the cosmos and my father will ever hand me in my entire life. There was a perceived danger. There were options for a peaceful solution. There were lives lost. Then despite being told it was too late, there were lives saved.

If there's any important lesson to this experience I would impart to you, it is this: No matter the size of the danger, no matter how large your fear, in order to make a difference you have to be strong. It's okay to be afraid, just remember to never let that fear hold you back. It's okay to feel hopeless, just never let it keep you from thinking outside the box. It's okay to be ignorant, just don't be afraid to learn.

Always do your best to never ever be too afraid to reach out with a piece of scrap paper and deliver the way to freedom.

Or hope.

A Little About the Tales

Silver—Written just before the fall of the Twin Towers, I was struggling as a single parent with my two small children alone in Bayonne, New Jersey. Being a country girl, I was often looked upon as "stupid" because of my accent and "plain" for my long black hair. Because I didn't know anyone there my life settled into a plain and boring existence where washing dishes was the highlight of the day.

Sometimes my friend, a spunky redhead, would ride the train with me into New York City. The one time we went to Central Park, I was blessed with the imagery needed to guide my lost feelings into this story.

This was printed in Kinships Magazine, but I don't remember the year.

> ***Over It***—*At the time this story was born, I was suffering a transition in my life. While trying to finish college in-between homes, I cared for the historic home of a famed pianist who lived in Springfield, Jacksonville, Florida while he was on vacation in Italy. Although he gave me permission to leave my homework on the table and to use their kitchen, his bookkeeper had a different opinion. Needless to say, I have a lasting opinion of her that could only be positively fueled into a fairy tale.*

It was published somewhere, but demmed if I can remember where or when.

Ghost in the Water*—This is a true story with a few embellishments, because a good tale always has conflict. In some manner or another, every event listed happened to me that day including the incident with the hair conditioner. I now always bring conditioner with me when I go swimming.*

In 2004 it was printed in the University of North Florida's *Nest Notes* annual publication.

The Glass of Cappuccino*—Once upon a time I had a best friend whose boyfriend was a manipulative jerk. I had no romantic interest in his person, but many people believed the opposite. If love could ever be misunderstood, it can with the woman labeled "fag hag".*

This story is about what it feels like to stand

on the sideline with only the power to make small wishes come true while the person you care about most in the world continues to wish for the unattainable.

> **For Fear of Breaking Hearts** - *This is a true story. I didn't even need to embellish. I just had to tell the story the way I normally would, knowing no one would believe me.*

I never forgot those poor bees, and I probably never will. I am adding it to this short story collection hoping that someone can take something away from the telling that's worthwhile.

www.ingramcontent.com/pod-product-compliance
Lightning Source LLC
Chambersburg PA
CBHW070445170726
48291CB00005B/1607